SQUEAKY CLEAN

*A Reluctant Feminization and Alpha
Billionaire Romance*

This book is dedicated to my fur baby, Snuggles.

He passed away on August 28, 2022.

Thank you for giving me 15 years and 3
months of unconditional love.

I will always love you.

Not to forget, YOU. The mere fact that you're
about to read this means that

you're part of the reason why I am blessed
to have a decent job amidst the

lack of opportunities for women like me in my country.

Thank you, from the bottom of my pink and girly heart <3

A Book By

LILLY LUSTWOOD

TABLE OF CONTENTS

SQUEAKY CLEAN
LILLY LUSTWOOD

INTRODUCTION

SQUEAKY CLEAN
LILLY LUSTWOOD

"From the billionaire's butler, she becomes the maid… but to clean her boss' chaotic puddle, she needed more than a mop."

Along with the browning of the leaves was the blossoming career of Mario Gomez, a 27-year-old butler who was up for a managerial position at the Luxor Heights hotel.

Enter Lance Oxford, a 28-year-old green energy prodigy who didn't only arrive at the hotel with his ego. With anti-Midas hands, he messes up Mario's pedantic lifestyle.

One fateful New York morning, Mario walks into the aftermath of Lance's private party, pivoting his life from purpose and organization to concealment and feminization.

Clutch your Pearl Necklace Tight and Prepare for a Transgender Romance Ride!

Note: This title contains feminization, transgender romance, transgender transformation, drama, and first time with a transgender woman tropes. Some real places and people were referenced but the story is a work of fiction. The cover image is from DepositPhotos and Lilly Lustwood.

I'm Lilly Lustwood and I'm a transgender woman. I'm a senior editor by day and I recall and write my romantic rendezvous by night.

Most of my titles deal with feminization. A fragment of what makes me find happiness in my gender identity, amidst the discrimination against women like me is my transformation.

When I look in the mirror and I gaze at my authentic self, I know that no matter what happens, I'm living my life and not somebody else's idea of how I should.

The clothes I wear, my long black hair, the fruity bath products that I use, the hormone medications

I take before I go to bed, the sillage of my floral perfume, the surgeries I've undergone, and every step that I take with my size 12 Jimmy Choos, are all proudly from me...

...from my authentic feminine self.

Picture this...

- ✓ I have long and straight black hair and stand 5ft 6in.
- ✓ My alabaster curvaceous physique enjoys silk dresses
- ✓ I'm blessed with huge cat eyes and heart-shaped lips
- ✓ My friends tell me that I look like Haifa Wehbe, Google her
- ✓ I want to share the rest but that's not very lady-like *wink*

It's January 08, 2023, and 02:12 PM in the Philippines. It's almost the second week of 2023 and I'm wearing a fun yellow dress.

Now that you know what your storyteller looks like, let's get to Squeaky Clean.

FREE VIP MAILING LIST

SQUEAKY CLEAN
LILLY LUSTWOOD

Before we get to the exciting part, I'm cordially inviting you to be a Lilly Lustwood VIP.

IT DOESN'T COST ANYTHING. All you have to do is Join my Mailing List.

I will be sending you FREE Exclusive Romantic Content that you won't find anywhere else.

My First Gift for You

Apart from that, I'll also send you Announcements of my New Releases and Promos.

I won't send you anything that's not related to my stories and I won't share your information with any person or entity.

CLICK TO READ FOR FREE

or Copy this Link -> stats.sender.net/

forms/er756a/view

Note: Please check your Spam or Promotions tab
if the confirmation doesn't arrive in your inbox.

Love Always,

Lilly

CHAPTER 1

SQUEAKY CLEAN
LILLY LUSTWOOD

The chambermaids and male servants, along with the housekeepers and butlers, gathered for an important meeting. Amidst the cool air that Manhattan's Autumn morning offered, everyone was sweating under their taupe uniforms at the Luxor Heights hotel's locker room.

"Lastly, Lance Oxford's coming".

What!?

"You might've heard of him. He's the solar panel *nepo baby*", Delia Cartwright, the 53-year-old brunette operations manager announced before pressing the creases of her black blazer.

"He's not demanding but he needs his room to

smell like *Dior Sauvage* at all times. Mario—".

"Yes mam".

"You know what to do. Kennedy Suite".

"I'm on it".

Moments later, there he was, Mario, in an all-black suit ensemble, fluffing the down-feather pillows in the Kennedy Suite's master bedroom. The oppressive three-bedroom accommodation housed a kitchen, a bar, a living room, and three bathrooms —and it was decked in chrome elegance and black modernity.

"Viv, can you restock the bar and make sure to get five bottles of *Hibiki* whiskey?" he requested after preening on the list that Delia sent on his work *iPad*.

"Yes! I mean, yes manager, haha!" Vivian elatedly said before dialing the hotel restaurant's line on the gilded telephone atop the chrome nightstand beside the California-king bed.

Vivian, the redhead maid, was Mario's closest friend at work. Along with sharing their love for killing bacteria, they also shared the same degree of disdain for Mario's rival, John Leong, a butler who enjoyed hogging the spotlight when it came to the attention of the higher-ups and esteemed guests.

Moments later, there he was, almost breaking the window wiper brought upon by his obsessive-compulsive nature. As the sun beamed on his earthy irises, soft tan, and short brunette locks through the squeaky clean glass window, he couldn't help but ponder his possible promotion.

His hope was filled to the brim as John picked the perfect time to get infected by COVID-19… during the visit of one of their most important guests of the year.

Manager…

As he clarified the view of Park Avenue in the living room, she started dusting the unused notepad and office tools that have been sitting on the maple study desk for a year.

"Do you think he's nice?" she queried.

"Who?"

"The solar guy".

"I really don't know much about him", he said as his obsession on the north side of the window trailed to the south.

"But I've read an article about how he became a billionaire by powering up malls in developing countries with his solar panels—he seems smart", he followed.

"Ha! If I had a daddy like Will Oxford, I'd be smart too", she jested.

"Yeah, that too. Haha!"

Shortly after, they moved to the master bathroom.

"Life's really unfair, he's like our age but he's already a billionaire, and here we are… about to wipe the bowl where he's about to shit on!"

"Don't worry, I'll rally for your promotion soon", he reassured with a wink.

Softly, he sauntered towards the toiletries trolly and picked up a bottle of Dior Sauvage perfume.

"Besides, these perks are not so bad", he added as he sprayed his suit abundantly with the citrusy concoction.

It was around past ten in the morning as they started scrubbing and wiping the white marble floors and walls of the master bathroom.

"Okay, so this is interesting, it says here that

he got a kidney transplant five years ago—", she informed as she scrolled through a *New York Times* article on her phone.

"—and that his sister gave it to him".

That's nice...

"As much as I love my family, I ain't giving anyone one of my kidneys", he said.

"I hear ya!"

Eww!

"Gross!" he let out as soon as he opened the metal trash can and saw more than ten discarded condoms filled with *babygravy*.

Squirming from the harrowing sight, he carried the bin in yellow rubber gloves and emptied the contents in the garbage trolley that was parked outside the bathroom.

It was past noon and the Kennedy Suite looked like it was freshly built. The fixtures gleamed, the rooms reeked of zesty *fuckboy* sillage, and the dust has been wiped to the tee. All that remained for the power duo to do was to fill certain areas with chocolate treats from *DeLafee*.

Moments later, there they were, in the reception

area with a backdrop of a gigantic carving of Cleopatra being fed with grapes by a male slave, awaiting the arrival of Lance Oxford.

As businessmen hustled and bustled in the lobby of the hotel that was decked in bejeweled Egyptian luxury, there he was, Lance, in a *Burberry* coat ensemble, blessing the guests with his enigmatic and immature charm alongside his hunky Samoan bodyguard slash driver who shared the same height of 6ft. 2in.

Oh wow...

"Welcome to Luxor Heights, Mr. Oxford", Delia greeted before tucking her hair behind her ear.

"I'm Delia Cartwright, the operations manager. This is Mario, your butler in the Kennedy Suite, and Vivan, the chambermaid. Please inform them if you need anything or simply dial zero".

"Okay", Lance said.

"Luggage", he followed without batting an eyelash.

Moments later, there they were, Mario and Vivian rolling ten of his silver Rimowa steel luggage bags with the bellman in the foyer as he smoked a cigarette on the black leather sofa in the living room.

"I thought he was an environmentalist", Vivan whispered.

"Haha! Shh! Maybe it's organic", Mario replied.

Annoyed by the indistinct chatter, Lance removed his sunglasses and glared.

"Fetu", he said—referring to his bodyguard.

"I know that you guys are assigned to this suite, but I like my privacy. Give me the extension number to contact you", Lance informed as Fetu handed them a hundred-dollar bill each.

Oh wow!

"Yes, sir, it's zero eight eight", he gingerly answered.

"Good. Now, scram!"

Feeling his heart beat a mile a minute from being treated like a stray dog, Mario trotted to the fire exit with Vivian and the bellman, Joe.

"Wow, he's really something!" he said.

"Yeah, a hundred bucks!" Joe replied.

"What a jerk! But wow! Ya'll better not tell the others!" Vivan interjected, referring to hogging the esteemed guest to themselves to bask in the *Benjamins.*

For some reason, Mario didn't feel insulted by Lance's treatment. If anything, it only piqued his interest in the haughty young billionaire.

CHAPTER 2

SQUEAKY CLEAN
LILLY LUSTWOOD

It was past eleven in the evening and the Kennedy Suite was filled with the sound of thumping speakers. In the room were two blonde runway models Anfisa and Lara, in their neon pink and blue two-piece lingerie, fighting over Lance's attention.

"What's this?" Anfisa queried after feeling the elevated scar on the side of his stomach.

"Don't you worry about that", he answered as he pulled her pink bra's strap down before kissing her.

"So, who was the guy with you earlier?" Lara inquired as she painted his back with soft kisses.

"You mean my bodyguard? That's Fetu".

"He's hot, ask him to join us".

Brimming with annoyance, he grabbed Lara's mouth and spat on it.

"Why don't you fucking make more lines? You cum slut!", he continued. Lance wasn't allowed to drink, and obviously, nobody was allowed to snort lines of cocaine. He signed a contract regarding his sister having the right to take her kidney back if she found out that he misused her generosity.

Albeit he trusted Fetu with his life, he knew that he would tell on him. The only loophole he could utilize was hiring hookers who would smuggle drinks and drugs for him. Whenever he traveled, Fetu always stayed in a separate suite adjacent to wherever he was.

The morning after, there he was, Mario, fresh from clocking in and drowning himself with the only scent that Lance allowed.

"Good morning, Fetu".

"Good morning", Fetu greeted back as he guarded his post by the oppressive oak door of the Kennedy Suite.

"I'm here to prepare his breakfast. I know that

he told me to scram last night but—".

"It's fine, he likes orange juice and pancakes".

"Thanks, Fetu, how about you?"

"I'll get something from the buffet later".

Moments later, there they were, Anfisa, Lara, and Lance, in deep slumber and lying naked on the floor in the living room.

What a night…

He tiptoed from the door by the study desk and ordered breakfast for three.

"Remember Luigi, don't ring the bell. Use the radio", he softly said before hanging up.

Because Vivian wasn't scheduled to clock in until two hours later, he started by cleaning the master's bedroom with the utmost discretion.

As he wiped the puddle of vodka and water on the tiles from the three's careless romp, an influx of doorbell rings started filling the suite.

Dammit! I told him not to use the doorbell!

Exasperated, Lance stood up and rushed to the peephole. There she was, Emily Oxford, his year-older sister, rolling her eyes from the delay.

"Don't you have a key!?" she queried.

"I'm sorry mam, I don't", Fetu answered in fear.

"Shit! Fuck!" Lance audibly whispered.

"Hide in the fucking closet! Take all your shit with you!"

As the two models wiped the drugs on the glass center table and picked their dresses and shoes to the walk-in closet…

"Oh!" Mario let out after they accidentally bumped into him.

Woah!

"Sorry", Anfisa said with a giggle.

"Fuck! Thank, God!" Lance said—as his flaccid *nine-incher* swung from side to side as he sprinted towards Mario.

Wowza!

"Hide the bottles and glasses in the closet and don't ever mention that I have girls in there! I'll give you everything you want!"

Without thinking things through, Mario started picking up the vodka and whiskey bottles and shot glasses on the floor.

Geez!

"Oh! And come back here as soon as you're done!"

With a heart beating a mile a minute, all he could do was nod and follow the naked billionaire's order. Moments later, there was Lance, in the pretense that he caught a cold as he burrowed himself under a thick white duvet on the sofa.

"Should I?" Mario asked—referring to if he should open the door.

Lance nodded like a troll and started letting out convincing coughing sounds.

"What took you so long!?"

"S-sorry madam, I was cleaning the bathroom…".

Emily scoffed and flipped the front layers of her blonde bangs to her back.

"Do I smell liquor!?"

Cough! Cough!

She inched towards her brother and investigated further.

"Did you fucking drink last night!?"

With feminine vigor, she tried to pull his duvet.

"I'm naked!"

"Eww, gross! Ugh! Why does it smell like alcohol in here?!"

Here goes nothing…

"Sorry about that madam, it's our new disinfectant. It gives off that smell. We're replacing it tomorrow", Mario lied as sweat trickled down his neck.

Soon after, Luigi, one of the hotel's male servants entered with a breakfast trolley.

"This is all for you!?"

Fuck…

"I can't talk too much, Em", Lance said with a faux hoarse voice.

"I-it's, the two plates are for the bodyguard, mam", Mario interjected.

Fetu, hearing the novel act of kindness, blushed.

"What do you want?"

"Mom asked me to pick you up for breakfast but looks like you wouldn't be able to make it. Does anyone have freakin' antibacterial wipes!?"

Mario rushed to the foyer and handed Emily a pack of unopened antibacterial wipes.

"Here you go", Mario said.

"I don't care if you're witnessing the apparition of the virgin Mary. The next time I ring the stupid doorbell, you open the door immediately! Got it!?"

Oh wow...

"C-certainly, madam. My sincere apologies".

With dagger eyes, she glared at Mario before making her exit.

Soon after, Fetu entered the suite in anticipation of his two plates of pancakes.

"Thanks, sir, I'm starving", he said.

"Yeah, take everything to your room".

Shortly after, there they were, Mario, standing idly in the living room as Lance pensively stared at the 7:30 AM Park Avenue view. Allowing the duvet to meet the floor, he shortly sauntered toward Mario —in full glory.

"Thanks, man. I owe you a lot".

"You're welcome, sir", he said—mustering all the courage his nerves had to avoid looking at the Eiffel Tower attached between Lance's legs and his body that was built like he was a modern-day Adonis.

"You seem like a good guy. My sister is a crazy bitch and I'm sure this won't be the last time she'd come barging in. About yesterday, forget about that".

You're both crazy...

"That's fine, sir".

"From now on, you'll be coming with me everywhere I go. Seems like you're the type who knows how to shut your mouth".

"C-certainly", Mario replied with an unsure tone and a face emanating the riddle of the Sphinx. Wanting to retort, he simply couldn't. His promotion highly depended on the billionaire's happiness.

"Good, order whatever you want for breakfast, I'll have what you're having. And please... get rid of the hookers in my closet", he said with a wink before hopping into the master bathroom for a hot morning shower.

CHAPTER 3

SQUEAKY CLEAN
LILLY LUSTWOOD

Half an hour later, there they were, Mario and Lance, enjoying a generous serving of *huevos rancheros* by the living room's floor-to-ceiling windows.

"I've never had this for breakfast. It's really good", Lance remarked as a dollop of tomato sauce landed messily on his white terry-cloth robe.

At that moment, it was Mario's very first time seeing how hypnotic Lance's eyes were—electric blue brilliance glowed gloriously under New York's eight-in-the-morning sunshine.

"My mom used to feed us huevos rancheros every morning. I wish I could have it every day but I don't have time to prepare breakfast anymore".

Lance reached for his glass—causing Mario to stand up and fill it to the brim with orange juice.

"Where's your mother?" the billionaire queried as he wiped the acidic mess on his chest with a table napkin.

"She's in Texas with my dad and some of my siblings".

"Interesting. We have a project down there".

Mario's butt found cushion on the black leather dining chair once more and proceeded to tear his bread.

"What kind? If you don't mind me asking".

"Nothing major. We're providing free energy for e-libraries where kids could connect to free Wi-Fi and... borrow i-Pads and use computers for free".

For real...

"I thought you...".

"Hmm?" Lance queried as he casually blew his nose on the napkin to get rid of the remnants of white powder that he sniffed profusely the night before.

"Nothing...".

"Tell me, or I'll tell the manager that you bought me drugs".

What the fuck!?

With eyes widened, all Mario could do was start calculating the right words.

"Haha, just kidding. So what were you about to say?"

With an aggressive swallow from the shock, Mario washed Lance's naughty blackmail with orange juice before clearing his throat.

"I didn't know you were helping children. I thought you were just working with corporations".

"Aha! In other words, you think I'm just some money-hungry jackass?"

"No! Absolutely not!" Mario let out as he shook his head like it was about to fall off his neck.

"Well, it's something to I guess... cover up the guilt I'm constantly hammered with".

"Guilt about what?" Mario asked—briefly forgetting about his boundaries.

"I'd like to share more about myself but you have to start first".

*If he wants me to cooperate, he
might as well do the same…*

"I'm up for a promotion and… serving you will play a huge factor in making it happen".

"Consider it done".

Oh my God…

"What I meant was, share something dirty about you. I'm great at keeping secrets".

Never did Mario imagine that he'd be rubbing elbows with people of Lance's stature. Not only was he rubbing elbows, but he was also seated across from him and sharing a lovely morning meal. In awe of how welcoming the billionaire was, he felt like the least he could do was follow his lead.

"I sometimes wonder if… I'd be happier if I were a woman".

With raised eyebrows, Lance leaned closer—causing his freshly calmed disposition frantic once more.

"I don't know, it's just silly. I just don't enjoy common guy stuff. You know?"

"I don't but you do you—".

"—erm, have you ever been with a woman?"

Oh God!

"Haha! No... I mean... I've never been with anyone", Mario gingerly informed—turning his caramel face further scarlet.

"Sorry, I think I've asked you enough. So, about me—".

"—my sister donated her kidney to me and I've been abusing it for many years behind her back. I really want to change but with my schedule and all, drugs and booze are the only things that keep me going".

Odd...

"And this", he followed before lighting up a cigarette.

"I think your sister did a noble thing. My dad used to drink and do drugs too in his twenties but he was able to recover".

"*Hoo...* How?" Lance queried with a face painted with curiosity.

"Love... I guess".

"Haha! That's funny", he continued before

tapping the ashes of his *Marlboro Lights* atop the chrome ashtray.

"Yeah, it's really corny but when he met my mom, he just quit—cold turkey. She gave him an ultimatum and he didn't wanna lose her".

"*Hoo...* well now that you say that, it kind of makes sense", Lance said as he puffed his curiosity away while staring at Mario's cat-like visage.

"Come with me to Buffalo, I have to make a speech".

"I'm not sure if I—".

"Your goal is to provide satisfactory customer service right?"

Mario nodded.

"And who's your customer?"

"You...".

"So come with me. I'll call Cassandra Mitchell".

"Okay, sir...".

"Just call me Lance".

"Okay, Lance...".

An hour later, there they were in the living

room, two female aestheticians in their all-white uniforms from New York's famous skin center, Cassandra Mitchell.

"Make him pretty", Frank said as he reviewed his green energy speech on the study desk in the living room.

What!?

"This is really not nece—".

"Remember your promotion", Lance interrupted.

The two ladies started unfastening the buttons of his black suit.

This is insane…

Shortly after, there he was, standing in full glory —giving Lance a view of his slim yet hourglass-like figure and tight bubble butt. Lance wanted to see more but the ladies led the nervous butler to the guest bathroom. All he could do was adjust his growing member and commence his review.

The ladies started by giving Mario a deep salt and volcano scrub. Too embarrassed by his *four-incher*, he covered his hairy crotch with his hands.

"What does this do?" he shyly asked.

"It basically gets rid of your dead skin cells. It helps the skin glow", Gina, the blonde aesthetician answered.

"What's that?" he queried once more, referring to a brown plastic bottle on the floor.

"It's Argan oil to make your hair voluminous and shiny", Sally, the brunette aesthetician informed as she started massaging his scalp with the imported shampoo.

Moments later, they started drying his body and heating wax.

"No! You don't have to do that!"

"Sorry but this is part of the treatment that Mr. Oxford booked".

"What treatment?"

"The *Barbie Skin* treatment".

"What the fu—I mean, what's that?" he asked once more—almost starting to irritate the ladies.

"So basically, it's a day-of prep to ensure that you're hairless and smooth everywhere".

Gulping from the harrowing hair-removal moment, he couldn't help but share his trepidation.

"But I've never been waxed before".

"Don't worry, we do thousands of these every year".

Feeling like they didn't want to hear another statement that ended with a question mark, with a deep breath, he closed his eyes and let the ladies commence their work.

"Ah! Ah!" Mario let out—bellowing the suite with his agonizing yells from the sharp pain brought upon by the ladies' removal of his leg, armpit, crotch, and anal hair.

Lance couldn't help but giggle from hearing Mario's expressions of the tormenting beautification process.

"Good morning, sir", Vivian said as soon as she walked into the suite.

"Good morning", Lance greeted back.

"Motherfu--!!!" Mario screamed once more.

"What's that sound!?" Vivian frantically queried.

"Is that Mario!?"

"Don't worry about it, he's just getting—", but

before Lance could finish his sentence, she rushed to where the seemingly torturous sound came from.

"What's happening here!?"

"Oh, hey Viv… they're, waxing me", Mario shyly said as he covered his hanging balls with a towel on all fours.

"Why?!" she whispered loudly.

"I'll explain everything later. You can start with the other bathrooms… Ahh!" he continued as soon as Gina pulled the wax strip from his butt cheek.

"*Yee-ouch!* Good luck!" Vivian said with a terrified visage before progressing with her assignment.

An hour later, there was Mario, with nothing but a white terry-cloth robe that was chaotically adorned with sliced cucumbers, standing by the study desk.

Lance couldn't believe how much Mario's face lit up from having his errant facial hair waxed and thick eyebrows threaded. Fully impressed except for one thing…

"You have a cucumber on your—", Lance said as he pointed at his right cheek.

"Oh!" Mario let out before picking up the sliced fruit and munching on it.

"Sorry about that…".

"Haha, that's funny. So, I prepared things for you to wear in my room. I have to be in Buffalo in two hours."

Huh!?

"But that's six hours away".

"You poor people are funny. Get to it!" Lance playfully ordered.

Moments later, there they were, Mario and Vivian, gossiping about what just happened as he wore the beige Burberry coat, cream turtleneck, white pants, and white sneakers ensemble that Lance has prepared for him.

"What the fuck is going on!?"

"I don't know either! I think he's bored and needs a friend."

"What's with the waxing and shit?!"

"Maybe some billionaire ritual? I don't know, Viv! I have to go! I'll text you later!"

Moments later, there they were, Lance, Fetu, and

Mario, on the hotel's rooftop.

"What do you think about his makeover?" Lance asked Fetu.

Perturbed by what he was referring to, he removed his sunglasses and peered at Mario's face.

"Something's different. He looks, cleaner?"

What the hell?!

"Right?" Lance followed.

Woah...

Moments later, there it was, Lance's gray private helicopter—blowing their coats and filling the air with the sillage of his favorite perfume.

"I'm scared...".

"What!?" Lance queried loudly to battle the resonance of the blades.

"I'm scared!"

"You're such a wuss! Come with me!"

Oh my God...

With Lance's protective handholding, Mario started experiencing novel feelings of butterflies dancing in his stomach. Reluctant from his fear of heights, all he could do was succumb and take the first step.

"At the back!", Lance said before scooching in with him.

"Is this your first chopper ride!?"

Mario nodded like a troll—squeezing his eyes in an effort to battle his anxiety. As the helicopter started taking off, all he could do was squeeze his hands in prayer.

Without thinking things through, Lance took his hand once more and interlaced his fingers with him.

Lance...

"Open your eyes! See how beautiful it is!"

Slowly but surely, with nothing but Lance's tight hold urging him, he marveled at the beauty of Manhattan from two-hundred feet in the sky.

"Wow! It is beautiful...".

"What!?"

"It is beautiful!" Mario screamed at the top of his lungs.

"It is...", Lance discreetly said as he gazed at

Mario's visage that was absent of adolescent curses.

CHAPTER 4

SQUEAKY CLEAN
LILLY LUSTWOOD

It was past nine in the evening when Mario and Lance arrived back in the suite. It was the very first time that the billionaire was able to deliver a speech and hold meetings without finding the need to take whiskey shots or snort cocaine beforehand.

For some reason, having Mario within close proximity provided him accountability.

"Thanks, sir, I mean, Lance, I really had a great time".

"Aren't you supposed to sleep in the suite?"

Oh, yeah...

"Oh, yeah, sorry about that. I thought you didn't

want an overnight butler".

"A butler, no, but a maid, yes".

What a player...

"After you shower, change into your uniform. I asked Vivian to buy some stuff for you. The bags are in one of the guest rooms".

Hmmm...

After a relaxing shower in the guest bathroom, there was Mario, damp and hairless, taking out the articles of clothing that his boss ordered for him.

What the fuck!?

As he held a long and wavy brunette, Lance entered the room, fresh off the shower with nothing but a green silk robe on.

"You don't like it?"

"You told me that you'd be happier as a woman", he softly said.

"I know but... not like this."

"Sorry but I can't—", but before Mario could exit the guest room, Lance pinned him to the wall.

"I'm not gay—but I want to kiss you. And I can't kiss you looking the way you do now", he said as he painted his butler's neck with warm breaths.

"I'm sorry but... I can't!" Mario retorted before pushing him away.

"Walk away from your happiness and your promotion!" Lance let out with a furious stare, stopping Mario in his tracks by the room's doorway.

Dammit!

Feeling like his knees were *Jell-O*, he fell to the floor with an influx of tears.

"I don't—".

"What about my family... what about my friends... If I start accepting this—", but before he could finish his sentence, Lance rushed to him and consoled him with a loving embrace from the back.

"What about you...", the billionaire said—tightening his hold.

Me...

Feeling Lance's guilt and warm embrace, Mario was powerless to retort.

"I'm sorry... you don't have to do it, just please... don't leave...".

Lance...

Shortly after, a warm rush coursed through Mario's body, causing him to brush Lance's arm and pick himself up.

"I think you're right... I guess it's about time", he unconvincingly said.

Mario inched to the bags once more and took the wig.

"I can't dress up while you're watching me... can you please leave for a moment?" he requested.

"Sure! I will!" Lance replied as he waited patiently in the living room.

Shortly after, there it was, the scintillating black French-maid uniform complete with an apron, a sheer two-piece nylon lingerie combo in the same color, white stockings complete with a lace garter belt, and four-inch black stilettos.

Slowly, he rolled the stocking on his smooth right leg, relishing the ticklish feeling that the fabric provided. Not knowing how to work the garter belt, he moved on to the other leg, basking in the warmth that it delivered.

It feels so nice...

Seeing his legs dressed in white stockings made

him appreciate how feminine his limbs were. Albeit not exactly a supermodel at 5ft. 6in., he had delicate and long strutters that were almost absent of masculinity.

So beautiful…

Gently, he removed the belt of his robe and picked up the nylon panties. Brushing the fabric, he couldn't stop his erection to grow. He wasn't sure if it was the forbidden act or the look of the underwear, but he knew that something was responsible for his excitement.

Fuck…

Soon after, there it was, his hard *four-incher* fighting the strict confines of the stretchable panties. Albeit a size smaller, she didn't feel uncomfortable as the texture offered a velvety feeling on his skin.

Feels so good…

With the bra in tow, he sauntered towards a wall mirror, in disbelief of his sight with nothing but black panties on and white stockings. He turned around and tried his best to hook the bra to no avail.

Wanting to ask Lance for help, he hesitated.

He didn't want Lance to see his boner. In fear of repulsing the billionaire with the sight of his member, he took a deep breath and tried to hook the back straps once more.

"Ahh! There you are".

So sexy...

Mario was far from a narcissist but his body was built for *Agent Provocateur* lingerie. His waist was tiny, his hips weren't wide, he had a bubble butt and his limbs were delicate. All he lacked was the protrusion that most lingerie models had in their decolletage area.

At that very moment, all of his reluctant thoughts blew away. What he saw in the mirror didn't only look right, it also felt right. Trotting to the French-maid uniform, he started wondering if Vivian knew that the uniform was for him.

Nobody should know...

Knowing that she was close to his parents, even if she was his best friend at work, he knew that his secret wasn't safe with anyone... except Lance.

Crouching to fit his body in the poofy uniform, he sprinted in front of the mirror once more. At that moment, he found out that zipping the back of a dress was just as hard as hooking the back straps of a bra.

"Ugh! This is a lot of work!"

However, his annoyance was soon flooded with awe right after seeing how the dress cinched his waist further with the tiny petticoat providing him an illusion of hips—intensifying his yearning to dress up more.

The only remaining items were the wig, the garter belt, and the shoes. Too excited to see his feminized look, he started with his crowning glory. After gently fixing his bangs, he placed the wig atop his head.

It was long, brown, wavy, and had playful layers, giving him a youthful and vibrant look. At that very moment, he wasn't looking at an image of a man anymore.

He didn't need cosmetics, all he needed was long hair.

Beautiful!

After gushing uncontrollably, he carefully slid into the right shoe.

"Ouch!" he let out from the pinching sensation brought upon by constriction. With unmitigable quivering, he stepped on the other pair.

This is amazing!

Not one waking moment did he ever imagine that he would stand beyond 5ft. 6in., but being in stilettos, he stood proudly at 5ft. 10in.

"Fuck!" he yelled as he stumbled in his tight shoes and almost twisting an ankle.

He may have suffered an injured toe... or two, but the spirit brought upon the novelty of his feminine self was intact. Slowly but surely, he strode once more, stepping on a tip-toe motion.

This seems like the way to go...

Once more, he preened in the mirror and marveled at his image. Without thinking things through, he picked up the garter belt and exited the room. With bated breath, he sauntered towards Lance who was eagerly waiting in a *manspread* in the dark living room that glowed dimly with the moonlight beaming from the floor-to-ceiling windows.

"I'm Maria, and I'm your maid for tonight. How

can I be of service?" he said with a wink.

CHAPTER 5

SQUEAKY CLEAN
LILLY LUSTWOOD

With bulging eyes and a heart that galloped, all Lance could do was stand up and draw Mario to him. The moment his hand met his waist, a shiver went down the maid's spine.

Lance...

"Wait...".

"Don't do this now, Maria", he said as he profusely painted Mario's neck with soft kisses.

"I've never been with anyone...".

Not wanting to endure the yearning anymore, Lance squeezed the novel maid's butt and lifted his leg—rubbing his hairy boner against his.

"And I've never done this with someone like you before", he mildly retorted before looking him in the eyes and offering Mario his first kiss.

Oh...

At that very moment, he discovered that all he needed in life to be sure about his sexuality was the billionaire's lips. Relishing the warm and fuzzy feeling that locking lips delivered, he tried to maintain his growing yearning. But feeling it rub against Lance's monster cock proved too deliriously delicious to bear.

"You have the softest lips I've ever kissed", Lance whispered before progressing to squeeze the maid's ass tighter.

"If it's not too late on your shift, I'd like you to clean something".

With a lascivious grin, he pressed his maid's shoulders and undressed his robe. Not knowing how to perform fellatio, all Mario could do was kneel and pray for the best.

As Lance's dick pulsated in a myriad of directions, Mario's cock bubbled with precum. Obliviously, the maid circled the billionaire's pink mushroom head with his tongue—driving his boss wilder from the pent-up excitement.

"Come on, Maria… you know you can do better", he let out before impaling his delicate mouth with his solid and girthy yearning.

"Gwak!" he let out as soon as Lance's cock knocked on his tonsils.

"Yeah…", Lance moaned as he relished his maid's warm oral embrace.

Tastes so good…

True to his hospitable nature, Mario tried once more to ensure that he provided the best service in the hotel industry. Enduring the choking and gagging, he let his tears flow and embraced his totality.

"Fuck!" Lance let out after releasing a bubble of precum. At that very moment, Mario's excitement heightened from having a taste of his billionaire juice, causing an insatiable hunger that he has never felt in his life before.

"I thought this was your first time".

"Gwak! Gwak!"

"I don't know what has gotten over me".

"Fuck, yeah…".

"We can't end it this way", Lance said before pinning him to the sofa.

He's so strong…

With every button that Lance unfastened, each beat from Mario's heart intensified.

"You're so beautiful, Maria…", he complimented with a lascivious gaze as he disrobed the maid of his uniform.

"You're amazing, Lance", he said with a scarlet face.

Gently, Lance lifted his stocking-dressed leg and started kissing his feet as he fed Mario with two of his girthy fingers.

"Mmm… mmm", Mario let out—locking the billionaire with his siren gaze.

"Fucking… hot!" Lance exclaimed before trailing his legs to his thighs with his mouth.

"What are you doing!?" Mario queried in exasperation as Lance started tickling his inner thigh with his tongue.

"I'm trying to return the favor".

No!

"You don't have to do that—".

Without thinking things through, Lance pressed his face against the maid's soiled black panties, displacing all of Mario's reluctant thoughts.

"Oh!"

"Mmm! Mmm!" Lance groaned like a bull as he shook his face in a playful demeanor—basking in the novel sillage of another person's testosterone.

"You smell very nice, I wonder what you taste like".

Lance pulled his panties down, revealing his extra-solid and pink *four-incher.*

"That's cute. I could work with that".

If there was a shade that was redder than red, it would be called, Maria.

"Mmm", Lance let out from relishing his first-time bout with a penis like he was trying out an exotic Mexican delicacy.

"Lance!" he moaned—on the verge of virginal ejaculation.

"I'm gonna cum!"

"No!"

At a hastened pace, he abandoned his penilingus practice and started kissing Mario once more. Moments later, he led him to the floor and started painting his back with warm smooches as Mario patiently waited on all fours.

"So tight!" Lance let out after spreading his ass cheeks and witnessing his hairless and pink hole.

Like a lion that hadn't had its meal for a week, he impaled Mario's hole with his tongue.

"Ahhh!"

"Mmm! Mmm!"

Hole-deep in euphoria, Lance bit his ass cheek as he gently stroked Mario's cock.

"You're so good, sir—I mean, Lance".

"Call me sir. Mmm, mmm".

"Okay, sir, please... keep doing that!"

"Mmm, mmm!"

Feeling satiated from rimming Mario's ass like there was no tomorrow, Lance started grazing his hole with his mushroom head.

Oh my...

"Maria, I know that this is not your job but I need you to unclog my pipe".

Mario wanted to burst into laughter but he didn't want to ruin the moment. With both of his heart and mind agreeing to provide the billionaire with the utmost satisfaction, he gently swiped his wig to the front and nodded.

"I'll do my best to satisfy you, sir...".

After generously spitting on his palm and lacing his nine inches of pleasure stick with saliva, he started invading his maid's ass like they were back in colonial times.

"Lance!" Mario let out from the agonizing sharp pain that his boss' penis provided.

Fuck!

As he squeezed his face to deal with the pain, Lance rolled his head in euphoria. Albeit having a playboy lifestyle, it was the billionaire's first time experiencing what it was like to enter an ass.

Possessed by the tactile sensation, he dared to insert two inches more.

Oh my God!

"Gahhh! Slowly, please!" Mario begged as he

squeezed the plush carpet on the floor.

Feeling Mario's ass made Lance feel like he was a virgin once more. Consumed by the warm and tight confinement, he sank his fingertips into his hips and inserted two inches more.

"Ffff!" Mario let out a guttural groan.

"Shh… shh…", Lance said as he inserted the very last inch of his seemingly neverending manhood.

"It's gonna be okay", he followed as he leaned in to kiss Mario's neck to calm him down.

"It hurts so much…".

"I'm sorry… shh…".

As Lance's Loch Ness monster freely pulsated in Mario's hole, the pain started fading away.

What…

Mario rose the white flag and briefly decided to ban bottoming in the future but at the very moment that his pain was rewarded with tactile sensations gifted by the harbinger of prostate pleasure, he curiously circled his hips.

"It's starting to feel nice, sir".

"Oh yeah?" Lance said with a grin.

Without thinking things through, he pulled his member out halfway and inserted his dick once more like he was playing with the Excalibur.

"How does that feel?"

Mmm, Lance...

"So damn good...".

Hearing Mario's declaration urged him to stab his virginity with his lance once more—completely eradicating all his stern heterosexual thoughts. At that very moment, they both gave in to the novel sensations brought upon by what they both considered taboo—affirming by filling the suite with the sound of their moans and groans.

"Fuck! Fuck! Fuck!" Lance let out like he was an infant who just learned how to say *mama*.

"Mmm! Yes! Yes!" Mario let out as he accidentally clenched his anal muscles—consuming the billionaire's dick with his hole that was as powerful as a *Dyson* vacuum cleaner.

"Ah! So fucking tight!"

"Ahh! Ahhh!"

I'm gonna...

"I think I'm gonna—".

"Let it out!" Lance cheered before sinking his fingers deeper into his hips and fucking him as deep as he could.

"Sir! I'm gonna—", but before he could finish his declaration, he messed up the floor with a puddle of cum.

Sore, satiated, and still enjoying Lance's dick, he let his cum drip and let his boss possess him.

"I'm gonna clean it later sir... sorry".

"I got something for you to clean now!" Lance let out with the veins on his neck looking like they were about to explode.

"Maria! Maria!"

"Sir!"

"Ah! Ahh! Ahh!" he let out, pounding the maid without care.

"Mmm! Sir, yes!" he cheered—almost causing the wig fall to the floor.

"Maria, fuck... Maria!"

With a tight grip, he performed his final push and opened his balls' floodgates.

"Fuuuuuuuckkkkkk!" Lance let out as Mario relished the warm and thick bath of unborn billionaire heirs flooding his prostate.

Feels so nice…

"Whooh!" he followed in a convulsive state.

"What have you done to me!?"

As soon as he released his very last drop, he unhinged from Mario's lascivious anal hold and rested on the floor. Gingerly, Mario rested his head on the billionaire's sweaty puffy pecs as he gazed at his exhausted yet satiated disposition.

So handsome…

"Thank you, Lance…".

With eyes closed, Lance kissed his maid's forehead and brushed his back.

"Thank you for your service", he jested before locking lips with Mario once more.

As they exchanged tongues like they were tying cherry twig knots, Mario started thinking about the possibility of exploring his femininity more—along with thoughts of whether or not Lance would continue helping him.

Stop!

Realizing that he worried too much, he decided to close his eyes, bask in the moment, and enjoy every tongue flick while he still had the billionaire with him on the floor.

CHAPTER 6

SQUEAKY CLEAN
LILLY LUSTWOOD

Being a butler by day and a maid by night made Mario, who's now Maria, feel unworthy of Lance's attention. After all, apart from the sex, what did they have in common, she pondered, as she fluffed the pillows in the master bedroom with Vivian.

I'm just a servant and he's a billionaire...

It was supposed to be easy for her to accept the modern caste system consensus, but with how deep the connection she has built with Lance in just three weeks, she couldn't fathom what made sense anymore.

"Mario—I mean, Maria, he's just like us, you know... human! Why don't you just stop worrying and have fun?".

"I don't know Viv, with this transitioning happening and sleeping with the boss—jeopardizing my promotion, and him...".

"Come here, look at me".

"You're not building a rocket ship. You're just living your life. Maybe it's the universe finally giving you everything that you deserve. Just... grab it by the balls and enjoy!" she said with a tight grab on her arms.

Viv...

"You always say the nicest things...".

"Ha! You know I ain't that nice!" she followed before pressing the creases of the white duvet.

Shortly after, they rested on the freshly-made bed as they stared at the ceiling.

"Where is he anyway?"

"He has an interview in the Stock Exchange", she said before trotting and preening in the wall mirror of the bedroom.

"By the way, we're running out on that Dior perfume thingy, please tell Marla to replenish the stocks".

The three postcoital weeks were a blur of many changes. Lance asked Maria to be his girlfriend and she slowly began her transition by getting used to being called Maria by Lance, Vivian, and her sister Lupe, and going by the pronouns she and her.

Albeit wearing a black suit ensemble at work, she ensured that beneath the masculine attire, her body was embraced by lingerie and stockings.

But it wasn't only Maria who was dealing with changes. Ever since Lance started dating her, he stopped drinking and doing drugs. Maybe she inherited the power to change a man from her mother, or maybe, he was just madly in love.

"Why don't you just take the kids with you to the suite? I'm gonna miss you so bad, babe", Lance said in a text message.

It was their very first night of separation as Maria needed to babysit her niece and nephew in the Bronx. Her sister Lupe, who was a single mother, needed to work overnight as a makeup artist for a fashion show that would be held in the wee hours for an up-and-coming eccentric fashion designer named Michael Sores.

"I'm gonna miss you too but I can't do that. I'm up for a promotion and these are the critical times when I have to be really professional. Think of this as an opportunity to miss me", she replied with a winking *emoji*.

It was past eight in the evening and Maria was basking in the compliments of her eight and nine-year-old *niblings* for her spaghetti Bolognese in her sister's dining room decked in cracked ecru paint.

"I wish you could sleep over more so we could have pasta every dinner!" Naya said before taking another bite of the meatball.

"Yeah, and we can play *Minecraft* all night!" Simon said.

"Haha! Your mother's gonna kill me if she knew that I let you play Minecraft on a Monday night! Don't you ever tell her!".

"How are you?" Maria texted Lance.

"I'm good, just waiting for my dinner. How are the kids?" he texted back.

"I'm feeding them now. I miss you so badly…".

"I miss you more, beautiful".

Lance…

Two hours later, as Maria and Naya watched Disney's *Encanto* in the living room and Simon continued creating a new world in Minecraft, there she was, Lupe, in her black leather trenchcoat, and her steel makeup train case.

"*Ayyy dios mio!*"

Lupe!?

As the kids trotted to kiss their mother, Maria rolled the sleeves of her black hoodie and helped carry her sister's cosmetics.

"Why are you home so early?"

"Oh my God, I was halfway done with the first model and Michael canceled the show!"

"What!?"

Lupe went to the kitchen and poured herself a glass of water as Maria eagerly waited to hear more.

"He said that he wasn't feeling the vibe tonight. Can you imagine that!?"

Maria shook her head in disbelief as her sister drowned herself in another glass of water.

"Did you at least get paid!?"

"Yeah, I was paid in full".

Seeing that it was only fifteen minutes after ten on her phone, she also poured herself a glass of water. It seemed that just like Lance, the idea of separation to miss each other didn't work for her as well.

"Do you mind if I go? I have to be in the suite".

"Sure, and thanks! But like, isn't it late?"

"It's our special client, you know I'm up for the promotion".

"Go get it, girl!"

"Shh! The kids don't know yet", Maria whispered in exasperation.

"Oh, sorry!"

Moments later, there she was, back in her black suit ensemble with a heart beating a mile a minute. Rushing to surprise her billionaire boyfriend with a box of her favorite New York pizza from the Bronx in one hand and the Kennedy Suite's key card in the other...

Fuck!

There he was, Lance Oxford, feeding a woman his white sausage in the living room.

"Ah… yeah… ah… Fuck!"

"What's going on!?" Maria yelled.

"Don't you know how to knock!?" Kelly, the blonde transgender bombshell that Lance met on *Tinder* said before sauntering toward the bar as her 36DD breasts and hard *seven-incher* swung side to side before taking a shot of whiskey.

"I thought you were at…", Lance said in a tipsy state as he tried to calm her by brushing her back.

"Is that alcohol I smell?!"

He leaned in to paint her neck with warm kisses but she pushed him away.

"Get off me!"

"I'm sorry, baby, I am… it's just that I really miss you".

"Is this like a threesome some?! You have to pay me extra for that", Kelly interjected.

"Just… get the fuck out!" Lance yelled.

"Relax! Where's my money!?"

"On the foyer! Get out!"

"Okay, geez!" Kelly replied before picking her clothes calmly from the floor.

"I can't believe that I've rushed here with a stupid pizza box to surprise you—".

Shaking her head as tears gently streamed down her cheeks…

"—turns out that you're the one who has a surprise for me!" she followed before throwing the box on the living room's window—vandalizing its earlier pristine condition with marinara sauce and melted mozzarella.

"I'm really sorry…", he tried to convince her once more.

"Did you fucking drink!?"

He shook his scarlet head in embarrassment.

"And I haven't been away for too long and you already found my replacement".

With an intent stare, she held his arms and forced him to look into her tearful eyes.

"What is it, Lance!? Is it because I don't have boobs!?" she asked before pushing his chest as he inched away to mitigate her fury.

"No…".

"Tell me! Is it because I'm not passable

enough!?" she pushed once more.

"No…".

"What!? What the fuck is it!? Why can't you be honest with me!?"

Not appreciating how cornered he felt in the foyer, he grabbed her arms with a harrowing gaze.

"You want me to be honest but you can't even be honest with yourself! Look at you! Look at what you're wearing! And all for a stupid promotion!?".

At that very moment, every word from her vocabulary escaped her brain. Not wanting to acknowledge how immature his thoughts were as to why she kept her gender identity a secret, all she could do was unhinge herself from his tight hold.

"I'm sorry… sir. I've crossed the line. I will send someone tomorrow to clean the mess".

Softly, she made her exit as he stared blankly at the floor with nothing but guilt coursing through his body.

CHAPTER 7

SQUEAKY CLEAN
LILLY LUSTWOOD

Lance stayed in the hotel for a week more and tried to contact her to no avail. Blocked constantly, he used all of his connections to find Maria. However, being that he was her first love and having experienced romantic betrayal for the very first time, all she could do was go *AWOL* and hide.

"Okay, this is really insane, you should forgive him! I swear, there are no girls in his suite and he hasn't been drinking!" Vivian informed Maria as they spent that particular Saturday night waxing each others' bodies in her living room decked in purple modernity in their matching pink terry cloth robes.

I can't...

"I don't know Viv, I'm not ready", she said as she applied cold wax on Vivian's legs.

"Delia has been looking for you. John has been hogging the spotlight again!"

"I'll talk to her when I'm ready.... John can get the promotion...".

Surprised to the core, all Vivian could do was eat the sliced cucumber slice atop her eye. After chowing down the other, she drew her attention.

"Girl... this is too much. I know how much you want that promotion. He really hurt you that bad huh?".

Maria, too somber to hide the pain, nodded and drenched her borrowed robe with tears.

"Aww... come here", Vivian let out as she encouraged Maria's exhibition of grief.

"Besides... he's a billionaire and I'm a maid. I'm also trans—".

"Again with—".

"—please, Viv. I don't need the pep talk. On what planet does a billionaire date a woman like me?

Seriously!?"

Vivian had her rebuttal ready but witnessing her friend's depression, all she could do was shake her head and provide her a warm embrace.

"You're probably right…".

A week later, Lance checked out of Luxor Heights as he had to stay in Silicon Valley for a month to deal with sharks. Maria, who has mustered enough courage to get fired, explained her conundrum to Delia about needing to start a new life as a woman over the phone, but to her surprise, the operations manager embraced her transition whole-heartedly—explaining the caveats of her abrupt absences and how they could affect her upcoming promotion.

It was six in the morning and the first day of snowfall in the city as some of the hotel's staff gathered in the locker room for a quick morning meeting. John, who couldn't help but gush about the possibility of him being promoted to manager, was elated to see Maria's new look.

As the staff of twenty controlled themselves to scurry and pry as to why Maria was wearing a wig and a black dress suit ensemble…

"Moving forward, please address Mario as Maria. She is now a woman and we should respect her identity. Use appropriate pronouns, and don't bombard her with questions".

"Thank you... Delia...", she shyly said.

"As for the new manager of the male servants —".

John scoffed and winked at Maria before proudly pressing his suit.

"Congratulations, Maria Gomez!"

Dios mio!

As the room was filled with the sound of applause, John couldn't help but feel his heart sink to the pit of his stomach.

"But... men should be in charge with the butlers!" he retorted.

Delia turned and slowly provided John with a displeased look—sending a shiver down his spine.

"Maria has clearly exhibited that she's more than capable of the job over the years of stellar work. Please cooperate... with your new boss", Delia followed.

At that very moment, all John could do was suppress his tantrum by blowing his black bangs away from his forehead. Too overwhelmed, all Maria could do was mouth *Thank Yous* as Vivian yanked her arm in excitement.

"I knew you'd get it!" Vivian said.

"By the way, Mr. Oxford told me to hand this to you", Delia informed as she passed her a folded letter.

"You can read it in your new office", she followed with a wink.

As Maria pensively gazed at the snowy Park Avenue view from her humble new office decked in white and oak modernity, Lance's letter started feeling like it was a truck of boulders. With a deep breath, she opened it to lift the weight off, curling her toes in her black *Mary Janes*.

"Dear Maria,

When you asked me the reason why, I had no answers. But now, I do. For a very long time, I've been doing things based on what felt good without acknowledging the feelings of other people... behind their backs.

I've been getting away with so many things for far too long and losing you just made me realize how much I needed to consider how others felt, even if they're aware or not.

I'm not sure if you'll ever read this letter but I just want you to know that whether you do or don't, everything that I've felt for you was real, and I know you've felt it too.

I'm still hoping that one day, you'd come to realize how much I love you.

It's not about the breasts, or how you look, or whatever. You're all woman to me. Don't feel otherwise because of my mistake.

Still crazy in love with you,

Lance".

At that very moment, all she wanted to do was book a flight to San Francisco, but also wanting to perform her best on her first day as a manager, she kissed the letter and tucked it safely in her breast pocket.

"Maria, please gather two butlers and proceed to the Fletcher Suite. Our guest is arriving at one", Delia said through the radio.

With an elated disposition, she assigned Bruno and John to the Fletcher Suite decked in blue and gold modernity as she rushed to the maintenance room to pick up additional cleaning supplies.

"Who's staying?" she queried on the radio.

"Some Jewish couple. The wife requested *Clean Fresh Laundry*".

"Gotcha".

Hours passed and it was around eleven in the morning and John hasn't uttered a single word to Maria yet. As he deigned wiping the floor-to-ceiling window under her supervision, she couldn't hide her emotions anymore. Softly, she started cleaning alongside his new subordinate.

"You don't have to do that, mam!" he said with an eye roll.

"It doesn't have to be like this, John".

With a scoff, he started rubbing the window, almost scratching the surface from disbelief.

"It's just so unfair, I've worked so hard... and here you are breaking all the rules."

"What rules? That male servants must only be led by men?"

"Yeah, and like, you went AWOL for more than a week!"

"I'm sorr—".

"Emergency! The guests arrived earlier than expected! Tell John and Bruno to clear the foyer and living room then proceed to the lobby immediately!" Delia announced over the radio in exasperation.

Moments later, there they were, the middle-aged couple in a matching beige *Loro Piana* coat ensemble, eagerly waiting to be led to the elevator.

"Good morning", Maria greeted before tucking her brunette wig behind her ear.

"Good morning, dear", the lady replied with a smile.

"I'm Maria, and I'm the manager of the butlers. These are John and Bruno. Please communicate with any of us if you need help. Let me lead you to your suite. Gentlemen, the luggage please".

"Oh, no dear, we travel light, we have everything we need in here", the lady informed as she rubbed the alligator leather of her brown *Birkin* bag.

Shortly after in the elevator, with newfound confidence, Maria pressed the button for the thirtieth floor.

"I have to smoke first", the lady said before pressing the button for the rooftop.

"You have a smoking room, madam".

"I don't like the smell lingering indoors", the lady's husband mildly retorted.

"Certainly, sir", John interjected—not trying enough to suppress his attention-seeking nature.

It was a white yet sunny Winter afternoon as the lady puffed the chill away while John got in a tangent of the hotel's history with her husband as Bruno scrolled through his *TikTok* feed on the corner of the rooftop.

"How long have you been working here?" she queried.

"About three years, mam".

"How do you like New York?"

The lady burst into laughter as soon as she heard what she thought was a preposterous question.

"Born and bred, darling", she informed before a long drag.

Shortly after, as Maria fidgeted from the

embarrassment of assuming that the lady wasn't from the city, the area was filled with the sound of a chopper's blade.

What the!?

"Delia, someone's landing on the rooftop", she informed on the radio as she led the lady away from the landing spot of the helipad.

"Oh, sorry, I forgot to inform you. Just welcome them, I'll be there soon".

"Okay".

As the sound turned inconveniently resonant and the vehicle started painting clarity, there he was, Fetu, shortly followed by Lance in a brown Burberry coat that he once loaned Maria.

Oh my God!

Soon after, a staff of thirthy started arriving, led by Delia to pry on the billionaire's arrival.

"Maria", he said.

"Mother, father", he followed.

What!?

The lady gave her a knowing smile before leading her to the center of the helipad. Gently, she passed a black velvet box to Lance and distanced herself from the two.

Without thinking things through, he knelt on one knee and opened the box. There it was, a five-carat round-cut *Harry Winston* engagement ring heirloom, shining brightly before her eyes.

"Maria…".

The crowd started drawing their cellphones out, including John to capture the moment. Vivian, elated to arrive just in time, couldn't help but yank John's arm in excitement.

"I don't know if you read the letter—".

"I have!" she said as her heart skipped several beats.

Lance blushed and softly giggled.

"I've never thought that I'd do something like this but ever since I met you, everything has changed. I like this version of myself best…", he followed as she wiped her tears of joy with her scarlet-polished fingers.

"You also brought a positive change in my life…", she replied.

"Let me explore those changes with you. Travel

alongside me… as Mrs. Oxford".

The crowd couldn't help but cheer Maria as they wiped their tears from the joy of witnessing what most deemed to be an odd pairing.

"Maria Gomez, will you please… please marry me!?"

At that very moment, it was her first time saying something without thinking.

"Yes!"

As the cool platinum setting romantically tickled her ring finger, he stood up and drew her to him.

"Oh, I love you, Maria, you have no idea how meaningless life was without you".

"I love you more, Lance. I'm sorry that I doubted your feelings".

"Oh, trust me, I have so many ideas on how you could make up for it!" he jested before locking lips with her as the Manhattan morning sunshine gloriously beamed on their true love.

EPILOGUE

SQUEAKY CLEAN
LILLY LUSTWOOD

Maria and Lance's relationship became the talk of the globe. Many people regarded their engagement as a modern Cinderella fairy tale.

Albeit grateful for the career opportunity, Maria filed her resignation and made a deal with John to get her recommendation. She made him promise to voice out the concerns of the workers about the salary raise and to ensure that Vivian would get better opportunities by serving important guests.

More than three months passed and they were still being photographed everywhere they went. Wanting to be the most beautiful bride on her wedding day, she decided to travel to Bangkok alone where she was scheduled for breast augmentation surgery.

Lance has completely gotten rid of alcohol and cocaine and created organizations to help medical research that could alleviate addiction and provide free gender-affirming surgeries for transgender people.

The End <3

Did you enjoy Squeaky Clean? In that case, I hope you could check out my first bundle Romantic Sissies Volume One.

It contains three sissification and feminization stories brought upon by domineering transgender women. In it, you will get six titillating books from the heart.

First Feminization Fiction - Modeling for Mrs. Morningwood

The first title follows the story of Danny, a lanky

high school senior who succumbs to a first-time feminization transformation brought upon by his first love for Mrs. Morningwood, a transgender woman who runs an adult publishing business.

Mrs. Morningwood finds out that Danny offered more than being a stand-in model. He reminds her that there was more to life than enduring a relationship with a cheating husband.

Second Feminization Fiction – Tokyo Sissy Hostess

The second title follows the story of Louie Liddledich, a travel vlogger who was determined not to take another dime from his wealthy father to pursue his passions. After several careless financial decisions, he stumbles upon a chance meeting with a Japanese transgender mama-san and loanshark who owns Tokyo's top sissy hostess club.

Discover how Louie swallowed his pride, ego, masculinity, and more *wink* in this forced feminization transformation and sissy training story.

Third Feminization Fiction – The Fifth Wife

The third title follows the story of Ahmed Al-Haziz, a multimillionaire tech magnate from a family of sheikhs in Dubai. With Amanda Cruz, his Asian transgender girlfriend's bubbling-up frustration from being treated like a holiday girlfriend, he was determined to prove her love to her by adhering to several conditions.

Amanda soon finds out that she bit more than she could chew after finding out that traveling to a middle-eastern country as a transgender woman was not exactly like a yellow cab ride. Just how will they be able to live as lesbian lovers with Ahmed's four wives and Amanda's immigration challenges in this sissy husband book?

Read Romantic Sissies Volume One

OTHER TITLES

"Transitioning, building a home, and being surrounded by sweaty workers proved to be a hard job."

Read Construction Site

It encapsulates five titillating reluctant feminization stories of men submitting to sissification brought upon by domineering t-girls and femdom.

Read Top T-Girls and Sub Sissies

It encapsulates three transgender romance and MM stories of three sissies' forced feminization fairy tales with dominant transgender women, *futas*, and romantic gentlemen.

Read Sissy Fairy Tales Volume One

Transformed By T-Girls Volume One is Lilly Lustwood's first collection of her Prima Femina Romances books.

Read Transformed By T-Girls Vol. One

Underneath her pencil skirt and silk blouse, distracting all the yearning men in the conference room with her apparition, she knew exactly who to give her attention to for her next career opportunity.

Read The Office Gurl

Find a place with utmost privacy and join
Lilly as she takes you back to 2007 when
she experienced being coveted, objectified,
and loved for the very first time.

Read My Cherry No More

"Vicious and criminally sexy, that's how they describe Stacey. Just how many notches on her bedpost should she accumulate to satiate her worldly desires?"

Read Stacey The School Sissy

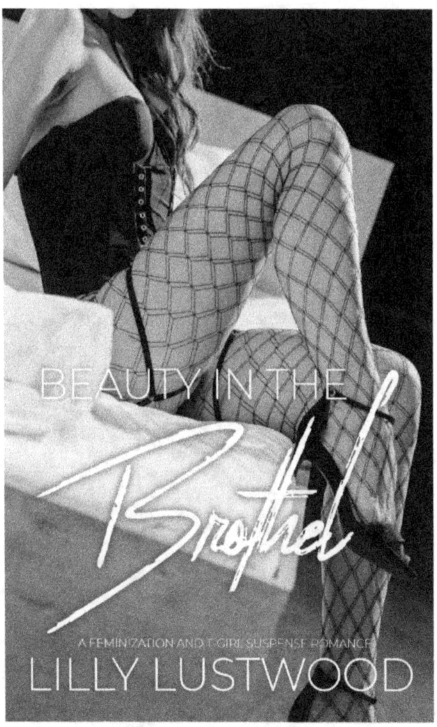

"In an underground T-Girl Brothel lies the dreams of transgender women, only to find out that they were all disillusions. Will her newfound beauty and bravery emancipate her sisters from the harrowing confinement?"

Read Beauty In The Brothel

AUTHOR'S MESSAGE

Dear Romantic Reader,

Thank you very much for purchasing and reading

Squeaky Clean – A Reluctant Feminization and Alpha Billionaire Romance.

For a writer, I can't seem to find the best word to describe how grateful I am for your support.

If you enjoyed this book, KINDLY (with puppy-dog eyes) give it a Rating and Review it on Kindle.

Let's get it to the overall bestseller list <3

Should you feel the need to send me a message concerning this book, your love life, or just about anything, please feel free to follow the pages below and Subscribe to my Mailing List to get updates on Free Books, Promos, and New Releases.

Mailing List (stats.sender.net/forms/er756a/view)

Home Page (www.lillylustwood.wordpress.com)

Amazon Page (www.amazon.com/Lilly-Lustwood/e/B0B9X11BMR/)

Facebook | Twitter | TikTok (@LillyLustwood)

Goodreads (www.goodreads.com/lillylustwood)